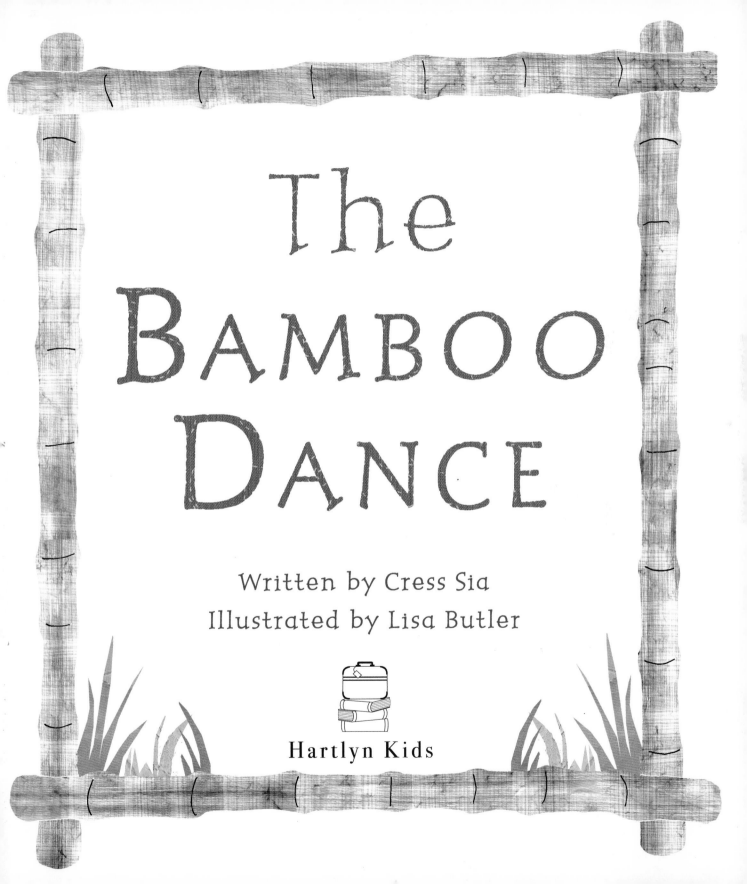

The
BAMBOO
DANCE

Written by Cress Sia
Illustrated by Lisa Butler

Hartlyn Kids

It is almost four o'clock on a quiet Tuesday afternoon and Paco's teacher is finishing today's lesson. Paco glances out the window at the beautiful day. Then he looks at the writing on the green chalkboard and down at his wrinkled notebook to take notes. Finally, the school bell rings. Classes are done for the day.

"Are you going home already, Paco?" asks Paco's best friend, Diego.

Paco looks around for his nanny, Nora. He shakes his head. "No. Nanny's not here yet. Do you want to go across the street and get something to eat?"

"Sure!" exclaims Diego. "I'm hungry!"

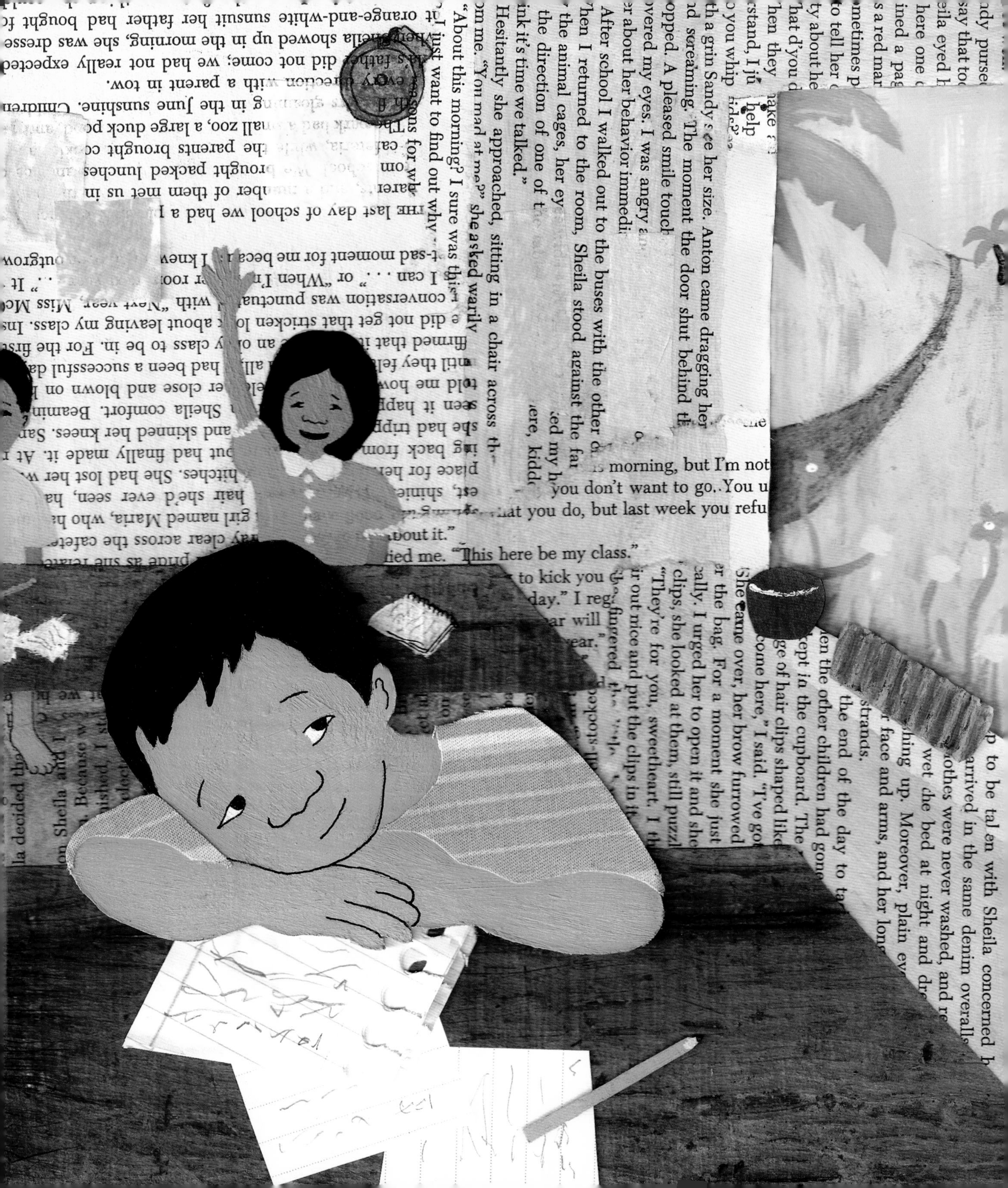

Together, Paco and Diego cross the narrow street to the strip of *sari-sari* stores. These are small shops in wooden buildings that sell a little of everything like food, soap, medicines, and other household needs.

Paco buys a stick of fried quail eggs while Diego purchases a piece of cooked banana dipped in brown sugar syrup. They each order a cup of sweet iced tea. Then they sit on a wooden bench outside the shop and eat silently.

Nearby, in an empty parking lot, Diego sees a group of children from their school gathering together. "Paco, look at them." Diego points at the crowd. "What are they doing?"

Paco looks intently at the crowd. The children circle around two dancers. The dancers, who are barefoot, stand between two bamboo poles that are laid on the ground side by side.

"I think they are going to dance the *tinikling*, Diego," Paco says. "Do you want to join them? We learned the steps last year in gym class, remember?"

"Yes, of course I remember," says Diego.

Quickly, the boys finish the last of their afternoon snack and make their way to the crowd in the parking lot.

Two older boys position themselves at each end of the bamboo poles. Each boy picks up the ends of the bamboos, one in each hand. Slowly at first, they tap the bamboo on the ground twice and up against each other once in a loud rhythm. Gradually, they quicken the beat. The dancers try their best to dance quickly without getting their feet caught between the bamboos.

"Let's dance, Diego," Paco exclaims. "This looks fun!"

A girl standing next to Paco says, "It is fun!" Paco recognizes the girl as a student who is a year older than him. "Next week, the town will hold an audition," she whispers. "Six dancers will be chosen to perform in the dance show for the *fiesta* next month. Everyone in school is eager to be a part of it!"

The *fiesta* is a yearly town celebration in honor of that town's saint. During the *fiesta*, everyone who lives in that town goes to the town center to eat, dance, and be merry. Streets are often decorated with hanging multi-colored flag banners. Families cook hearty meals and invite friends and relatives over to eat.

Diego's eyes widen. "Being part of the dance show? Wow!" he says.

"Come on, Diego! Let's see if we stand a chance!" Paco says, already beginning to take off his black leather shoes and white socks. The dusty road tickles his bare feet, and the blazing sun warms his skin as he waits for his turn to dance. Finally, Paco steps between the bamboo poles and sighs.

"Here I go!" he tells himself. Soon, Paco is skipping and dancing beautifully to the beat of the *tinikling*.

As soon as the dance ends, Diego and the other children applaud.

"That was well done, Paco!" Diego exclaims.

Paco wipes the sweat on his forehead and bends over to put on his socks and shoes.

"It's your turn now," he says to Diego.

Diego grins excitedly. He is the last one to dance. He takes off his shoes and socks and steps between the bamboo poles. At first, Diego's feet move with ease and grace. But then, as the beat speeds up, Diego becomes agitated. It is as if he can no longer move his feet fast enough while keeping the next step in mind.

Soon his feet are caught between the bamboos. Diego hears the crowd yelling.

"Boo!"

"That boy can't dance!"

"Let's go home!"

One by one, the crowd turns to leave. The older boys holding the bamboo poles eventually put them down. One of them says to Diego, "You don't stand a chance, boy."

Diego moves away from the bamboos and bends down to put his socks and shoes on. Paco can see tears building up on Diego's eyes. Paco gently pats his friend's back.

"It's okay, Diego. I will help you with your steps. You will be a good dancer in no time."

Diego gets up and looks Paco straight in the eye.

"No, Paco. Didn't you see? I just embarrassed myself! I will never be good at that stupid dance!" Diego wipes away his tears and walks away. "I'm going home!" he yells.

Paco stands near the parking lot and watches Diego walk away. Soon Paco sees his nanny, Nora. He runs to hug her. She smells wonderful, like fresh lemons and eucalyptus.

"How was your day, Paco?" Nora asks.

"I can't believe I still remember the bamboo dance, Nanny, and I can dance it so well too! If I keep practicing, I might be chosen to dance in this year's *fiesta*!" he exclaims, skipping the *tinikling* steps gleefully in front of Nora. "But Diego seems to have a hard time," Paco says, stopping his little demonstration. "And he thinks he will never be a good dancer."

He takes Nanny's plump hand and together they walk to church.

"Maybe you can help him with his steps, Paco," suggests Nora. "Every day after school, you two can practice together."

"I want to help him, Nanny. But I'm not sure Diego wants me to. The other children put him down pretty badly today."

Along the way, Paco sees a little girl selling small leis of fragrant *sampaguita* flowers. He stops to buy two leis. Paco smells their sweetness. The flowers are so small and delicate that Paco holds them very carefully.

The church near Paco's school is centuries old. Statues of saints decorate its grand altar.

Upon entering, Paco dips his fingers in a small well of holy water and makes the sign of the cross. He lays one lei in front of an image of the Virgin Mother Mary. Paco believes a woman as virtuous as she deserves only the purest and whitest flower—the *sampaguita*. Silently, Paco bows his head and tells her of the events this afternoon after school. He asks Mother Mary to pray for Diego and himself. Before they leave, Paco remembers to bow and make the sign of the cross.

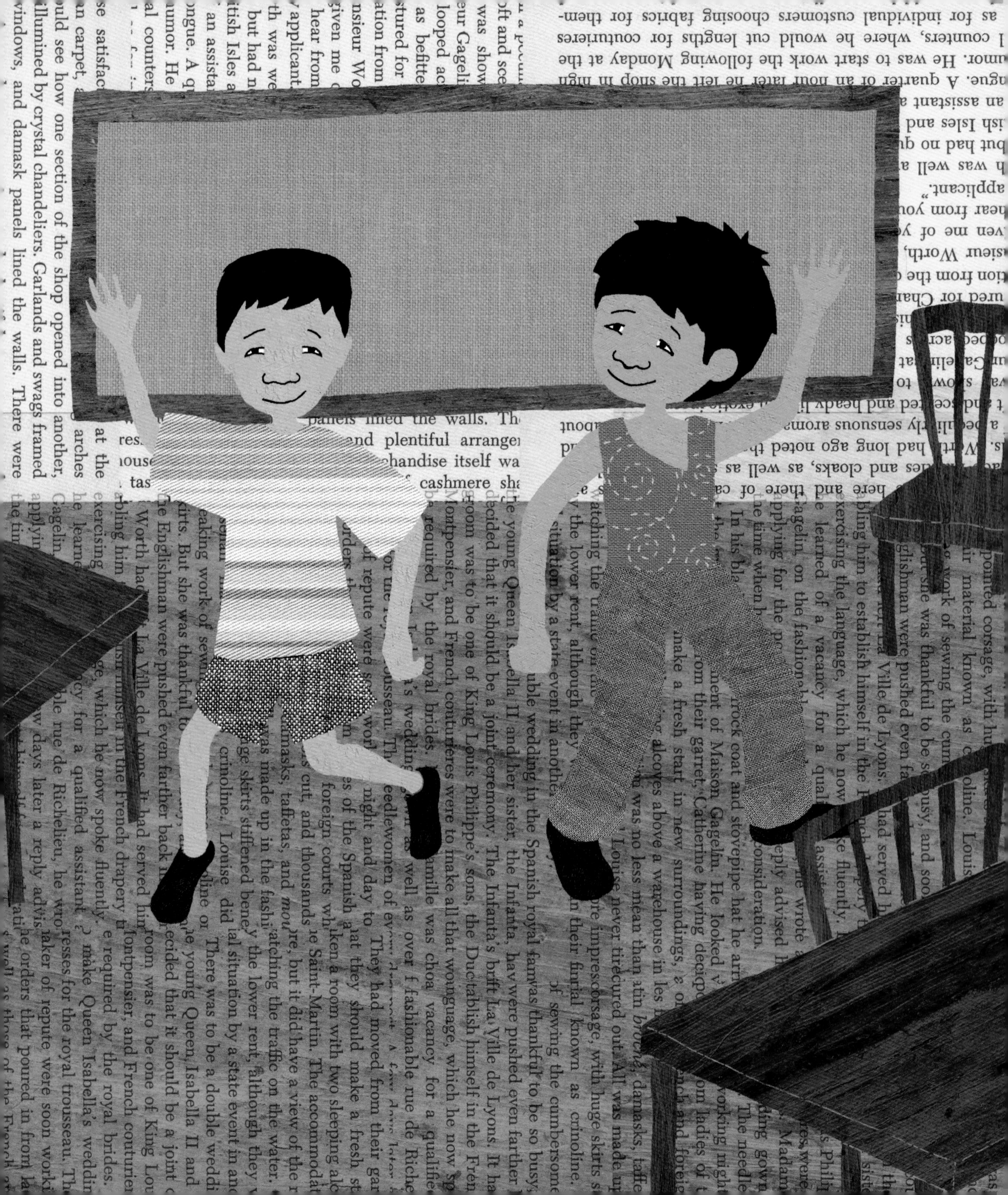

The next day in school, Diego avoids Paco. Paco can tell that Diego is still very upset about yesterday.

As soon as classes end, Paco catches up to Diego and walks next to him. "I'm really sorry about what happened yesterday, Diego," Paco says.

Diego shrugs. "It doesn't matter," he says. He doesn't look at Paco.

"I can help you with your steps," Paco encourages, hopeful. "In fact, why don't we practice right now? We can go back to the classroom. Nobody is there."

Diego stops walking and looks at Paco. "Do you really think I can dance it well, Paco?"

Paco smiles. "I know you can!"

Diego grins, and the two of them hurry back to the classroom.

Every day for the next week, Paco and Diego practice the bamboo dance. On the first day, the boys dance slowly side by side so that Diego can get used to the stepping. The next day, Paco picks up his speed just a little so that Diego can catch up. The day after that he speeds up a little more. At first, Diego stumbles a lot. But he doesn't give up. And before Diego knows it, he is dancing the *tinikling* almost as fast as Paco.

Finally Diego feels confident enough to dance outside. He and Paco go to the parking lot where other children have been practicing. Paco and Diego line up and wait for their turn to dance.

Finally, it is their turn. "Come on, Diego," Paco says. "Let's dance together." Diego hesitates, but at Paco's encouraging look, he walks with him to the poles.

As soon as Diego steps between the bamboo poles, a few children start to jeer at him. "Look! It's the little boy who can't dance!" someone yells. Paco looks at Diego. He can sense his friend tensing up.

Diego feels so anxious that for a moment he feels his body freeze. He continues to hear rude remarks. "Don't waste our time, boy!" someone scoffs.

"Don't listen to them, Diego," Paco begs. "Believe in yourself!"

Diego closes his eyes and shakes his head to clear his thoughts. He has practiced for days. He can do this. At Paco's signal, the older boys holding the bamboos start tapping them to the ground and up against each other, slowly at first before building up to a furious beat.

Paco and Diego skip perfectly together to the bamboo dance, from start to finish. The crowd quiets down as they watch the beautiful show, their mouths agape. Contrary to what they have been thinking, Diego, the boy who can't dance, is now dancing brilliantly!

On the day of the audition, it comes as no surprise that Paco and Diego are both chosen to dance in this year's *fiesta*. Diego has learned how to dance the *tinikling*. And he has also learned a very important lesson, and that is to believe in himself!

LEARNING TOOLS

TINIKLING: the national dance of the Philippines. The tinikling is
an indigenous dance from the Philippines that involves two
people beating, tapping, and sliding bamboo poles on the
ground and against each other in coordination with one or
more dancers who step over and in between the poles in
a dance.

SARI-SARI stores: small shops in wooden buildings that sell a
little of everything, like food, soap, medicines, and other
household needs.

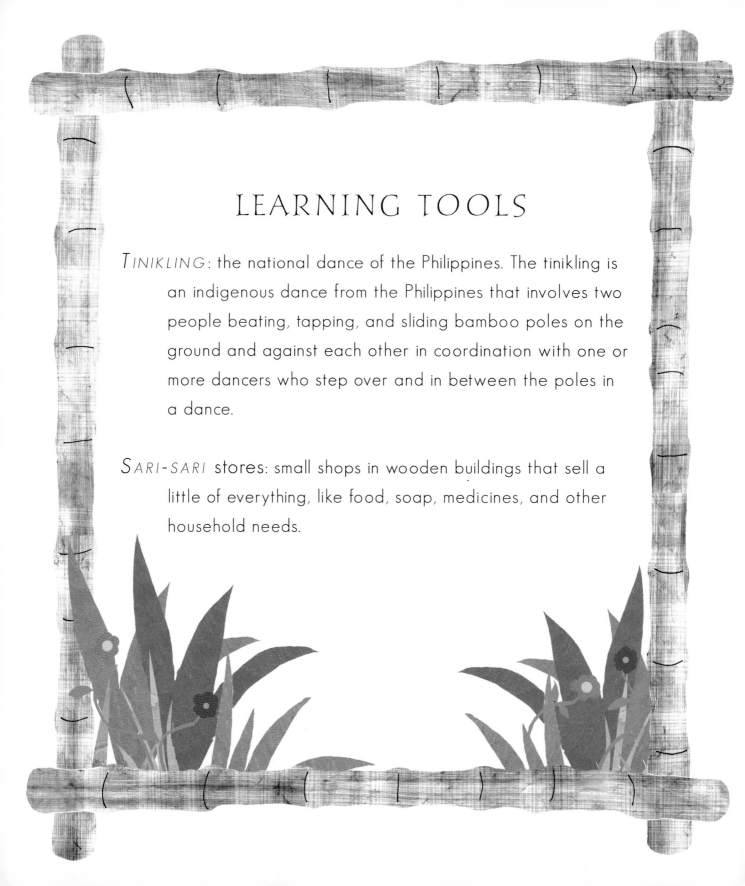

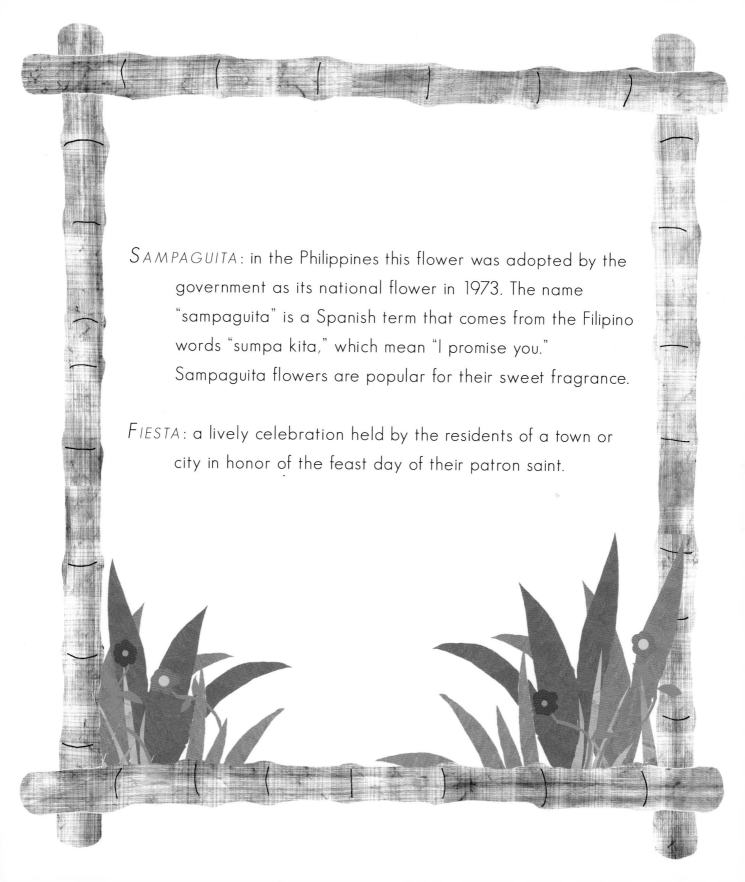

SAMPAGUITA: in the Philippines this flower was adopted by the government as its national flower in 1973. The name "sampaguita" is a Spanish term that comes from the Filipino words "sumpa kita," which mean "I promise you." Sampaguita flowers are popular for their sweet fragrance.

FIESTA: a lively celebration held by the residents of a town or city in honor of the feast day of their patron saint.